The Boxcar Children Mysteries

THE MYSTERY
IN THE MALL

created by
GERTRUDE CHANDLER WARNER

Illustrated by Charles Tang

SCHOLASTIC INC.
New York Toronto London Auckland Sydney
New Delhi Mexico City Hong Kong

ISBN 0-439-05608-X

12 11 10 9 8 7 6 5 4 3 2   9/9 0 1 2 3 4/0

Printed in the U.S.A.   40
First Scholastic printing, September 1999

Contents

THE MYSTERY IN
THE MALL

CHAPTER 1

Monkey in the Middle

At a rest stop by the side of a road, the Alden family sat around a picnic table. In the middle of the table, next to their picnic basket, sat a coconut. This was not an ordinary coconut but one painted to look just like a monkey. Six-year-old Benny Alden had carried it all the way back from Hawaii on another family trip. Now the coconut monkey went with him everywhere.

When lunch was over, Benny picked up his coconut by its rope handle. He shook it to hear the rattle inside. Then he took the last bite of his banana.

"You look just like that monkey," fourteen-year-old Henry told Benny. "Especially with that banana."

Benny held the monkey coconut next to his freckled face. He made the same monkey face, too. "Can you take a picture of me, Violet?" he asked his ten-year-old sister.

Violet found her camera. She aimed it at Benny and his coconut. "Say cheese."

"Yip! Yip!" Benny said instead.

After Violet finished taking Benny's picture, Grandfather Alden stood up. "There's nothing I like better than a roadside picnic. Mrs. McGregor outdid herself with this lunch. Everything tastes better out in the fresh air after a long car ride. Now it's time to get going again."

The children cleared the picnic table.

Henry gathered up two bags of trash from around the picnic table. "Take nothing but pictures, leave nothing but footprints," he said. "Violet took the pictures, and I'm leaving nothing but footprints. This trash is going right into the Dumpster."

While Henry went off, Jessie spread out a map. She was twelve and the best map reader in the family. She always knew where they were and where they were going. "It's not too much longer, Grandfather. See, we're here, about an hour away from Hope Harbor."

"It'll be nice to see my friend Martin Bolt," said Grandfather. "Not to mention the new mall he's built! He said you children will have a very good time there."

Benny was excited. "I heard the mall is right where all the boats come in! I can't wait to see that."

"So you will," Grandfather told Benny.

"I took out that trash just in time," Henry said when he returned. "A garbage truck just came to pick it up."

"I'm glad we stopped," Violet said after everyone repacked the car. "It's so pretty here."

"And I'm glad we're not stopping again.

This sure is a long car trip," Benny complained. "Whoops! Don't leave yet, Grandfather!" Benny said. "I forgot my car bag under the picnic table. It's got my travel games and toys in it — my coconut monkey, too!"

Benny raced out. From the car, the rest of the family could tell that Benny's bag was nowhere around.

When Benny returned, Henry gave him a friendly arm punch. "No luck, huh? I'll check the trunk. I bet you anything your bag is back there."

Henry got out and opened the trunk. When he came back, he was awfully quiet. "I hate to tell you this, but I think I made a bad mistake. I thought the shopping bag under the picnic table was trash, not your car bag. A truck just drove away with our bag of trash and your bag, too, Benny."

The children stared down at the empty highway. The truck had disappeared, taking Benny's coconut monkey with it.

"I'm really sorry, Benny. I should've checked both bags before I tossed them out," Henry said.

"It's okay, Henry," Benny said. "Maybe I can get another coconut monkey if we ever go back to Hawaii."

Mr. Alden drove for a long time before any of his grandchildren spoke up again.

"We're here!" Jessie announced an hour later, waking up the other children, who had finally dozed off.

When Benny opened his eyes, he saw a big sign on a building that said HOPE HARBOR MALL.

"See, Benny. We made it," Jessie said.

Benny sat up straight. He felt better already. He liked everything he saw. Crowds of shoppers strolled along walkways that zigzagged along the outside of the mall building. Seagulls swooped down to catch french fries tourists tossed out at them. Hope Harbor Mall looked like fun.

"Wow!" Benny said. "I never saw a mall on a big dock before. It's bigger than Main Street in Greenfield."

Mr. Alden searched for a parking garage. "Martin built the mall right on the water so shoppers would enjoy the view of the harbor."

Violet perked up when she saw all the shops that opened onto the pier. "I'm glad your friend's mall is indoors and outdoors, Grandfather. I like to be able to see outside."

"Same here," Jessie said. "Usually I can't tell if it's day or night in a mall. Hope Harbor Mall is different."

Mr. Alden drove through the underground parking garage. "Martin Bolt grew up in Hope Harbor. He built the mall to bring people back to the waterfront. Before he rebuilt the docks and put the mall on one of them, the whole area was just falling apart."

"Not anymore," said Benny. "It's busy around here, with boats and people and seagulls and lots and lots of places to eat."

Grandfather laughed along with Henry, Jessie, and Violet.

"You just finished Mrs. McGregor's picnic lunch," Jessie teased. "How can you even think about food?"

Benny smiled. "Because I smell food —

all kinds. French fries, caramel corn, hot dogs, and pizza!"

Mr. Alden soon found a parking space. "Here we are."

The children locked their things in the trunk. Everyone trooped out and followed signs that said THIRD-LEVEL STORES AND OFFICES.

Mr. Alden opened the parking garage door to the light-filled mall. "Just look at this view."

Down below lay the bustling waterfront of Hope Harbor.

Benny ran over to the huge glass windows. "Tugboats! I love tugboats. They're small, but they push around big barges."

"Like you push me around, right?" Henry said, teasing Benny.

At that moment, a tall, thin man with straight gray hair came up to Benny. "Move away from that window. If you want to see the boats, you'll have to go out to one of the walkways."

As soon as Benny moved away, the man

took a paper towel and rubbed the window.

"I didn't lean on it," Benny said. "See! No fingerprints."

"Humph," the man said, polishing the clean window anyway.

After the man left, Benny turned to Grandfather Alden. "I didn't touch the window. I just looked at the boats."

Mr. Alden put his arm around Benny. "I know that. Sometimes older folks like us forget what it's like to be children."

"I'll never forget," Benny said. He stayed a good distance from the big picture window now.

"There's Martin's office," Mr. Alden told his grandchildren when they reached the end of the long hallway. "You'll get a view of the harbor on all sides from there. Let's go in."

Violet and Benny joined their grandfather. Henry and Jessie stayed behind, reading a bulletin board.

"Come on, you two!" Benny said. "What are you reading, anyway?"

Jessie caught up to the others. "Help-wanted signs. This mall is hiring people to work here."

"Greetings, Aldens!" a cheerful-looking man said when the Aldens came in. "So these are your grandchildren, James. I've heard all about the four of you. Your grandfather has mentioned so many times how lucky he was to find you after your parents died. He's told me how well you took care of one another and that you lived very snugly in a boxcar. Now I have the pleasure of meeting all of you in person. This is quite a treat."

The children liked Grandfather's friend very much. Martin Bolt even looked like James Alden, tall and silver-haired and just about the same age. Mr. Alden introduced the children.

"I bet you like boats," Martin Bolt said when he noticed Benny glued to the window.

Benny nodded. "I like boats, but somebody didn't like me looking at boats. He thought I got my fingerprints on your windows, but I didn't."

Mr. Bolt just laughed. "I'm sure you

didn't. And even if you did, I wouldn't mind. The view is there for the looking. Now, I hope you young people plan to stick around Hope Harbor Mall while your grandfather and I go to our college reunion. Just enjoy this place. I could use some young folks like you to tell me what you like and what you don't like, so I can keep my customers happy."

"We saw all the jobs posted on the bulletin board down the hall," Henry said. "Since you asked what we like, we like working. That's what keeps *us* happy."

"Work on a vacation?" Martin Bolt asked. "Nonsense. You children are my guests. Mrs. Frye, my housekeeper, will set you up in my house. The top rooms are fixed up just like cabins on a ship. You'll have a fine view of the harbor, and it's just a few minutes from the mall. I want you to have fun."

Mr. Alden laughed deeply. "You don't know my grandchildren, Martin. Work *is* fun for them. If you have anything at all that needs doing around here, my grandchildren would love nothing better."

"Hmmm," Mr. Bolt said. "I've got a good idea of a store where you could work *and* have some fun. Let me check with my mall manager, Hap Merchant, first."

Martin Bolt came back a few minutes later. "Hap is on his way over to meet you. Tomorrow morning, he'll bring you to Penny's Emporium, a shop that just opened. Hap's been helping out Penny Block there while she breaks in a new store manager. But I need Hap for other things. If Penny has some extra helpers, Hap can get on with his other jobs."

At that moment, the grouchy man who had scolded Benny stepped into the office. Seeing the Aldens didn't make him any more friendly.

"This is my manager, Hap Merchant," Martin Bolt told the Aldens. "Hap, meet my good friend James Alden and his four grandchildren. Oldest to youngest, they're Henry, Jessie, Violet, and Benny. I thought they could give Penny a hand with her new shop. That will free you up a bit."

Hap Merchant ignored the Aldens' outstretched hands. "Well, I don't know that Penny needs a bunch of kids running loose in her shop."

Mr. Bolt's smile disappeared for a second. "Now, Hap, I want you to know the Aldens have worked in stores before. If James Alden tells me they're hardworking, I know Penny will be tickled to have them."

Everyone noticed Hap Merchant's frown. Mr. Bolt waved him into a back office. The Aldens could hear the low, serious voices of the two men. A few minutes later, Martin Bolt and Hap came out. Hap brushed by everyone, then left.

"Sorry about that, James," Martin Bolt said. "If I let him, Hap would run the whole mall by himself. I can't have him spending so much time at Penny's shop. I need him to supervise workers all over the mall. Anyway, he'll call you children tomorrow at my house to give you the details."

"Let's hope Hap Merchant is friendlier to us tomorrow," Jessie whispered to Henry. "I wonder if he'll really call."

CHAPTER 2

A Mixed-up Day

The next morning, Benny woke up to the sound of tooting. He kicked off his covers and went to the window. Down in the harbor, a red tugboat tooted again. Slowly, it pulled a barge away from the dock.

"Henry," Benny whispered. "Time to get up. Come look outside."

Henry opened one eye, then the other. "Where are we? Why are there round windows in this room? Are we on a boat?"

Benny pulled off Henry's covers. "We're

in Mr. Bolt's house. The windows are round, like on a boat. Come look outside."

Henry pulled the covers over himself again.

"You're no fun," Benny complained. "I'm going to wake up Jessie and Violet."

Benny tiptoed down the hallway. The floor creaked. When Benny opened the door to his sisters' room, that creaked, too. Mr. Bolt's house was like an old, creaky boat.

Violet stood at the window. "Hi, Benny," she whispered. "Look, there's a tugboat pulling a barge. Come see."

"I saw it already," Benny answered. "Can we go down to the docks before we go to the mall?"

"As soon as we get dressed," Violet told Benny. "Jessie and I will meet you and Henry downstairs in ten minutes. I think Mrs. Frye already has our breakfast started. I smell bacon."

"There you are!" a cheerful older woman said when the Alden children appeared in the kitchen doorway.

"Good morning, Mrs. Frye," Jessie said. "We didn't need an alarm clock to wake us up. The sun reflecting on the water came right into our room."

"And boats tooting. That's my alarm clock," Benny said. "It's hard to sleep with all that tooting going on."

Mrs. Frye laughed as she set out breakfast for the children. "After a while you don't notice the tooting. I'm glad there's no phone on the top floor, or you would have been up even earlier when it rang for you."

Henry poured milk on his cornflakes. "Did Grandfather call already? He and Mr. Bolt only left last night."

Mrs. Frye poured herself some coffee. "Oh, the call wasn't from Mr. Alden. It was Hap Merchant. He said to go off and have a good day and not to worry about working at the mall until he calls again."

"Gee, I think Hap might be mixed up," Jessie said. "He was supposed to tell us when to meet him at Penny's Emporium. We'd better get this straightened out."

Mrs. Frye came around with a pile of

toast. "We're just a few minutes from Hope Harbor Mall. No need to rush off. Why you children want to work when there's so much fun to be had, I just don't know!"

Benny reached for another piece of Mrs. Frye's buttery toast. "We *do* know. We like jobs. That's our fun."

"We'd better talk with Hap in person," Jessie said. "Then we can explore."

The Aldens helped Mrs. Frye with the breakfast dishes. She loved their company. While the children scraped and washed and rinsed the dishes, Mrs. Frye told them all about how Mr. Bolt had brought back the wonderful seaport of Hope Harbor.

"Now that the mall is here, the boats unload a lot of freight right off the docks for all the stores in the mall. Hope Harbor Mall is different from most malls. The stores sell things from all over the world. Just last week at Penny's Emporium I found a lovely plate from Switzerland."

Benny seemed worried. "Does Penny's shop just sell little china dishes and fancy kinds of stuff like that?" he asked.

Mrs. Frye laughed. "Not to worry. Penny's is the perfect place for children to shop in or work in. You can do both. Penny's shop has everything — candy, a caramel corn machine, souvenirs, and balloons. There's even a corner in the shop where folks stick their faces behind a pirate cutout and have their pictures taken. You'll find toys and souvenirs from all over the world. Penny gets her goods from Asia, Europe, Hawaii."

When Benny heard *Hawaii*, he made his silly monkey face. "I had a coconut monkey that had a face like this. It came from Hawaii, only not on a boat. I carried it all the way back on the plane."

Mrs. Frye laughed. "Did you eat your coconut monkey?"

"Not that kind of coconut. It was a big coconut shell with a monkey face painted on it. I bought it with my own money. They had pirate coconuts, but I like monkeys. I lost it when we drove here. It went into a garbage truck by mistake."

Mrs. Frye patted Benny's head. "What a

shame. Well, you must tell Penny Block about it when you meet her. I've never seen coconut monkeys in her shop, but I bet she'd know where to get one. Now off you go, children. I'll leave a message at Penny's shop telling her to expect you. Take your time getting there. Penny doesn't open up her shop until ten."

On their way to Hope Harbor Mall, the Aldens had plenty of time to walk along the waterfront. Several freighters were unloading at the docks.

"I wonder what's on all those boats," Henry said. "Some of those freighters come from far away. That one says 'Tahiti' on it. See, Benny? That's far away, like Hawaii."

"Hey, look! The police are checking one of the boats," Benny said.

The other children looked up. A man and woman in blue uniforms followed a young crewman with curly black hair from crate to crate on a small freighter. They poked around, checking some of the boxes and taking notes on their clipboards.

Benny grabbed Henry's arm. "Maybe the crewman is really a pirate! What if there are stolen jewels inside one of those boxes? Will those police put him in jail?"

Jessie laughed. "We've all been reading too many mysteries to you, Benny! Those aren't regular police. They're customs inspectors. Customs people check goods that come into the country from other countries."

Benny noticed that the inspectors checked some boxes but not others. "Well, they're not doing a very good job. They skipped some boxes."

"Let's get a little closer," Henry told Benny. "The inspectors can't check every single thing, or they'd never finish. They just pick boxes at random. The shippers have no idea which boxes will get checked."

"Maybe that's why that crewman looks so nervous," Benny said.

"Is this the last of the shipment?" one of the inspectors asked the crewman.

The young man shifted from one foot to the other. "As far as I know, that's all of it," he answered. Then he dropped the screw-driver he'd been holding. When it started to roll down the gangplank, Benny raced to catch it before it fell into the water.

"Thanks," the young man told Benny. "Good catch."

Finally the inspectors drove off in a government car they had parked on the dock.

The young crewman watched the car pull away. He yelled down at the Aldens. "Hey, you have to leave, too. Tourists aren't allowed on this loading dock."

The children looked at one another. The docks were open to anyone.

"He's not very nice to us," Benny complained. "And I even caught his screwdriver."

Jessie checked her watch. "I guess we should get going. It's almost ten o'clock. I wonder if some of the shipments they just unloaded are going to the mall."

The children started to walk away. Benny turned around to wave at the crewman. But the crewman didn't wave back. He was busy lifting up some kind of trapdoor from un-

der a huge coil of rope. The young man pulled out some boxes, counted them, then put them back under the trapdoor. He looked around, then threw the rope over the door. From where the Aldens were standing, there was no way of telling that the crewman had a secret hiding place. The customs inspectors had missed it completely.

CHAPTER 3

Look Who's Minding the Store

"What are you sniffing, Benny?" Jessie asked when the children stepped inside the mall.

Benny kept his nose in the air and didn't answer Jessie right away.

"I know. Benny's sniffing for caramel corn, right?" Henry asked.

Benny made a face. "How come I don't smell any? Yesterday I did."

Jessie pointed to the huge clock in the middle of the food court. "It's morning. People eat breakfast, not caramel corn, in the morning."

"Shucks," Benny said. "Mrs. Frye said there would be caramel corn at Penny's shop. Let's go look there."

The mall wasn't too busy yet. The shopkeepers were setting up for the day. They rolled up their security gates. Some of them set out pushcarts of small items to sell in front of their stores. Cleaning people pushed mops and brooms to make the mall spick-and-span for the day.

"Look who's coming down the hall," Violet said to the others.

"Uh-oh," Henry said. "Hap Merchant doesn't look too glad to see us here."

Hap looked puzzled, then annoyed when he noticed the Aldens. "I thought you kids would be sightseeing today. I left a message for you with Mrs. Frye. Did you come here to shop?"

"We're going to see Penny Block," Henry told Hap. "Mr. Bolt wants us to work for her, remember?"

Hap didn't look at all pleased to hear this.

"Well, I'm the mall manager, and I'm sure Mrs. Block doesn't need a bunch of children running around like little monkeys."

"We wouldn't do that." Jessie hoped Benny wasn't going to make one of his monkey faces while she was trying to be serious.

At that moment, an older woman with wild curly red hair and wearing a bright purple blouse and funny eyeglasses came up to the children. "You're the Aldens, right? Mr. Bolt called me last night and told me to keep an eye out for two boys and two girls. Here you are, and just in time. One of my shipments is down on the dock. I need a strong young person to bring the boxes into my storeroom."

Hap tried to say something, but Penny Block was like a runaway train. "Anyway, if you haven't guessed already, I'm Penny Block. We can get acquainted while we work. I have a list a mile long if you children are ready to work. Let me show you my shop."

Before Hap could squeeze in a word, Penny rounded up the Aldens. The group went off, leaving Hap behind.

Penny's Emporium was designed to look like a seaside shop on a boardwalk. In one corner stood a tall tank of helium for blowing up balloons. In another area, a camera was set up to take pictures of people who stuck their heads through a funny pirate cutout. A caramel popcorn machine took up another corner.

"The rest of the shop is for souvenirs," Penny continued. "If any of you is good with your hands, I could sure use you to wrap gifts for our customers."

Violet was too shy to say anything, but Jessie spoke up for her. "Violet is the best one in our family for wrapping presents."

"Then you can be my chief gift wrapper, Violet," Penny said. "I had a feeling you were the one for that."

"What am I the one for?" Benny asked.

Penny Block laughed. "Why, our caramel machine, of course. I need a careful boy to scoop the caramel corn into boxes. Folks come in here all day for Penny's Caramel Corn. My husband, before he died, always told me the way to bring folks into a shop is to sell something that smells good. They'll come in for that and go out with a Hope Harbor teapot or a dish towel. And he was right."

"Mrs. Block, have you ever seen a coconut painted like a monkey? Mrs. Frye told me you might sell them," said Benny.

"I know just what you mean, Benny. I'll keep an eye out for them at the gift show I'm attending this afternoon."

"Great! Thanks a lot," said Benny.

"What can Jessie and I do?" Henry asked.

Penny pulled out a pad of paper. "A lot, if you aren't afraid of work. I need somebody to be in charge of taking pirate photos. They're very popular souvenirs with tourists. Jessie, you would be good to sell souvenirs from my pushcart in the mall area. That gets people to stop in front of my store. Henry, you're my gofer. Go for this. Go for that. Is that okay with you?"

"I'll go for it!" Henry joked.

Penny showed Henry where to find the hand truck from the storeroom. She needed him to pick up some boxes at the warehouse.

Just as Henry headed out the back door of the shop, a young woman came in. "Where are you going with that hand truck?" she asked Henry. "That belongs to this shop."

For a second, Henry was lost for words. "It's . . . uh . . . well, Penny said I should . . ."

"Who are you?" the young woman asked. "Penny didn't tell me anyone else was working here. I'm the store manager."

At that moment, Penny stepped into the storeroom. "Hello, Janet. I see you've met Henry Alden. You know how you said there was so much to do? Well, a miracle happened. Martin Bolt sent the Alden family to save the day. Henry, this is Janet Trainor."

The young woman ignored Penny's introduction. "Mr. Bolt sent children to work here? That's not going to be much of a help at all. I can't work with children underfoot."

"Nonsense," Penny said. "The younger ones have already started. Henry is on his way down to the warehouse to pick up a shipment that came in. You can go ahead, Henry. Now, come meet the other Aldens, Janet."

Benny was at the popcorn machine, carefully scooping caramel corn into boxes.

"He's going to make a mess!" Janet told Penny. "And why is that girl wrapping packages?"

Penny was very patient. "Violet Alden is wonderful with her hands. I have her wrapping some of the gift plates. You know how much time that takes. Now you'll have more time to wait on customers."

The young woman sighed deeply. "I guess I'll go out and load up the souvenir cart, then. Wait! Where is it? I pushed it just inside the door last night before we closed."

Penny smiled. "Take a look out there.

Jessie Alden already stocked it. I posted her out there to wait on customers who are passing by. You can cover the shop. I'm heading to the gift show at the convention center. I feel much better about leaving now that the Aldens are here to do all the little jobs."

After Penny left, Janet shadowed the children around the shop. She expected them to do things one way: her way. She rewrapped a package Violet had already wrapped perfectly. She stood over Benny to make sure he didn't drop one kernel of corn. She checked up on Jessie, who had already sold several souvenirs without anyone's help at all.

Soon Henry returned from the warehouse with a stack of boxes. "I'll get a box cutter and open these if you want," he told Janet.

When the young woman saw the boxes, she grabbed the hand truck from Henry. "I'll take those, thank you. I'm going to lock them up until I have time to match everything against the order slips."

Henry smiled. "I could do that if you — "

Janet shook her head. "No, it isn't as easy as it looks." With that, she rolled the hand truck over to a storage closet and locked the boxes inside.

The day passed quickly. At five o'clock, Benny tapped Henry's elbow. "Is it time to go, Henry?" he asked. "Penny said we could leave around dinnertime. I like it here, but now I'm hungry."

"Sure thing, Benny," Henry answered. "I'll go find Janet. She's in the storeroom again."

Henry found the young woman scrambling through the boxes he had delivered that morning. Janet wasn't alone. Standing next to her was the dark-haired crewman the Aldens had met on the dock that morning.

"Hey, aren't you — " Henry began. Janet and the young man turned around suddenly, startled to see Henry standing there.

"What are you doing here?" Janet asked,

quickly shoving the boxes inside the closet again. "I was . . . uh . . . telling this man where the blue jeans store is. He wandered in here by mistake."

"Sorry." Henry wondered why the crewman had come into the storeroom to get directions. "I just wanted to let you know my brother, sisters, and I are leaving as soon as Penny gets back."

Janet's eyes were dark with annoyance. "You don't have to wait until Penny gets back. I've covered the shop by myself before."

Henry backed away. Why was this young woman so grouchy all the time? "Okay," Henry said. "Oh, well, there's Penny now. I guess we'll go." He looked at the crewman again. "I just figured out where I saw you — on the freighter this morning, right?"

The man turned away from Henry without answering. He opened the back door of the storeroom and left.

Penny suddenly appeared in the doorway. "I'm back, and you won't believe what I found out at the gift show, Henry. My supplier says there's a whole shipment of novelty items on one of the ships in the harbor right now, including — guess what — coconut monkeys, coconut pirates, and coconut clowns! Once they're unloaded in a few days, I'll set aside one for Benny just as soon as I open the boxes."

Everyone was smiling at this good news, except for Janet.

"What's the matter?" Penny asked the young woman. "Don't you think we could sell a lot of those? You look as if I told you we'd be selling dead bugs."

"Oh, it's . . . uh . . . nothing," Janet said. "I'll unpack the boxes as soon as they get here."

CHAPTER 4

Monkey See, Monkey Do

The Aldens joined other strolling tourists on their way to the mall's many outdoor restaurants. At sunset, people liked to come outdoors, look at the view, and eat outside.

Jessie checked the directory of all the shops and restaurants in the mall. "Mr. Bolt said the Dockside Café is a good place. It has tables inside and outside."

"Look, Benny!" Henry said suddenly. "Those seagulls like to eat outside, too."

The Aldens watched screeching seagulls

36

swoop down for french fries that people held out for them.

"There's a couple leaving soon," the restaurant hostess told the Aldens when they arrived at the jam-packed restaurant. "You can have their table as soon as they leave and the busboy clears it."

The children studied the menu posted nearby.

"I'm having french fries just like the sea-gulls, only I want mine on a plate," Benny decided. "And chicken fingers and carrot sticks to go with the french fries."

While the other children decided what to have, Benny watched the couple. He hoped they weren't going to order any more food. Luckily for Benny, they got up to leave.

"Hey, it's Janet," Benny whispered to Jessie.

The older children turned to look.

"Right! And that crewman is with her again," Violet noticed.

Henry tried not to stare. "Put your heads down. I don't want them to know we saw them. I forgot to tell you that the crewman was in the storeroom. Janet told me he was lost. Doesn't it seem funny he's having dinner with her now?"

Jessie peeked, then looked away from the couple. "Did he say anything about seeing us on the dock this morning?"

Henry shook his head. "That's the thing. As soon as I mentioned it, he walked out the back way. Also, I was wondering why he went out the back of the store if he was lost."

"Your table is ready," the restaurant hostess said, interrupting Henry. She led the children over to their table.

"Goody," Benny said, settling into his chair. "We're right by the railing so we can watch the seagulls."

Violet laughed and pointed to the sky. "And the seagulls can watch you, Benny! Look how they fly over all these outdoor restaurants. Better watch your food when it comes."

Benny took one last look at the menu. "When my food comes, it won't be on my plate long enough for the seagulls to get it."

Benny was right about that. He ate every bite of food and still had room for dessert. While he waited for his brownie sundae, he found a piece of paper under the saltshaker. "Hey, look." He showed the note to the other children. "I wonder who left this. The handwriting says: *'Checklist: Appt. SS Shop; Check all boxes. R.T.'* "

"If it said 'J.T.,' then I'd say that was Janet Trainor," Jessie said, reading the note. "Well, a lot of people eat at this restaurant. I guess we'll never know who R.T. is."

When Benny's brownie sundae arrived, he stuck the note in his pocket and forgot about it. It was time for dessert.

"That was a good dinner," Henry said later after they paid their bill. "I have a couple of things to do. I'll meet you all at Penny's shop at nine o'clock. She'll tell us whether she needs us tomorrow or the next few days."

Jessie pulled Henry away from Benny and Violet. "Where are you going? Are you going to snoop around down on the dock?"

Henry shook his head. "No, even though I want to," he whispered. "I'm going to see if I can find another coconut monkey for Benny. I feel rotten that I threw his out by mistake. There are so many shops around here with stuff from all over. Maybe there's a chance I'll find one. It could take a long time for Penny's shipment to arrive."

Jessie smiled. "That would make Benny so happy. He hasn't complained once. Well, good luck. We'll meet you back at the shop around closing time."

"What are you and Violet whispering about?" a tired Benny asked when he caught his sisters giggling secretively. "And why won't you tell me where Henry went?"

"We can't tell," Violet said. "Now let's do some more window-shopping."

An hour later, the children strolled back to Penny's Emporium. Henry was already there and wearing a huge smile.

"You beat us," Benny said when he saw his brother.

Henry held out a brown shopping bag. "I did more than that. Look inside."

When Benny looked down, he saw something round and brown and covered with hair. "My car bag with my monkey! Yippee! Did that garbage truck come to Hope Harbor, too?"

Henry laughed. "Nope. Take a look inside. It's not the car bag or exactly the same monkey as the one you lost, but it's from Hawaii, or at least that's what the store owner said."

Benny reached into the shopping bag. He felt for the rope handle and pulled up the coconut. "Ta-da!" He held the coconut next to his face and copied the same grinning face.

"It's close enough to the one you lost," Jessie said. "Shake it."

"That's exactly what I did," Henry said. "It was the last one in the store. As soon as I saw it, I decided to buy it. I made sure it rattled just like Benny's lost one. Go ahead, Benny, shake away."

Benny shook the coconut. "Now I can make a racket with this one, too."

By this time, Penny had locked up the cash register. "Well, I'm awfully glad you found one. Who knows when the coconut monkeys I ordered will get unloaded?"

Penny and the Aldens heard the storeroom door bang.

Janet came into the shop area. She noticed Benny's coconut right away. "Where did that come from?" She looked at Penny. "I thought you wanted me to open all your shipments, Penny, so that things wouldn't get mixed up. If everybody does it, we won't be able to keep track of our stock."

"Relax, Janet," Penny told the young woman. "Henry found that one in another shop. He didn't want to wait for our shipment. How was dinner at your mother's?"

Janet looked confused and didn't answer right away. "Oh, it was fine. I just got back."

The Aldens looked at one another. They didn't know whether to say anything. What if Janet had changed her plans and didn't want to bother telling Penny? It wasn't their business to keep track of where Janet ate dinner.

Penny checked her watch. "Gee, look at the time. The security people will be coming by to scold me. All the shops must be locked up by nine-thirty."

Everyone heard a *putt-putt* sound getting closer. Hap Merchant drove a motorized cart right up to Penny's shop. He flashed a spotlight into the store. "Closing time, Penny."

"We're just shutting down, Hap," Penny said. "We were having a little gathering for Benny. His brother found a present to replace something he lost."

When Benny heard this, he picked up his coconut monkey and shook it by the rope handle.

"What a racket!" Hap said. "Rules are rules. It's closing time. You kids need to go home. I'll come back and take you to the parking garage, Penny."

Quietly now, Penny switched off all the lights to her shop. "No, thanks, Hap. I'm going to walk the children out and give them a ride home." She pulled down the security gate. The last thing the Aldens heard was the click of the lock and Hap's motor cart heading down the dark hallways of the mall.

CHAPTER 5

Benny's Good Idea

Benny and his new coconut monkey were a big hit the next day. Several of Penny's customers asked whether it was for sale. "No way," he answered with a cheerful smile.

Benny's monkey even came to the rescue when a little girl came in to have her picture taken for a pirate picture. Henry did everything he could to make the girl smile, but she wouldn't put her face behind the pirate cutout.

"Come on, Katie, stay still and smile for

the camera," the little girl's mother said.

But the little girl wouldn't smile. In fact, every time she looked up at her mother, her lip trembled as if she were about to cry, not smile.

"Oh, dear," the mother said. "We were going to get a pirate photo for her dad's birthday."

Henry made funny faces. He held up a teddy bear. But the little girl kept getting up and running to her mother.

Benny figured out just what to do. "Wait a minute, Henry. I've got an idea." Benny placed a stool next to his brother. "I'll stand next to you and hold up my monkey. I'll make faces. That will make the little girl laugh."

Sure enough, as soon as the little girl saw the monkey's silly face and Benny's identical silly face, she sat still and gave the two boys a big, dimpled smile. Click! A perfect picture.

Pretty soon, there was a line of customers who wanted pirate pictures, too. "With the monkey, okay?" some of them asked.

So Benny lent out his monkey. But he was very careful to keep an eye on it. One little boy's dad offered Benny ten dollars for the monkey.

"It's not for sale," Benny said.

"I'm expecting a shipment in a few days," Penny told all the customers who wanted coconut monkeys. "Make sure to come back."

"You children have worked enough today," Penny said later on. "Didn't you tell me you had some shopping to do at the mall? The stores close soon, so why don't you leave now?"

Jessie and Violet finished wrapping last-minute souvenirs for several senior citizens who had to get back to their bus.

"Grandfather gave us money to get new jeans before we go back to school," Jessie told Penny. "That jeans shop next door has a lot of them. I guess this is a good time to go shopping."

It was never a good time for Benny to go clothes shopping. He wanted to go to the store that sold nothing but train models. Or go window-shopping at the store that had puppies in the window. Or stay at Penny's and show off his monkey. Anything but clothes shopping.

"Come on, Benny," Jessie said. "We might as well get it over with. You're growing like a tree all the time. Look how short your jeans are."

Benny looked down. About two inches of his socks showed between the bottom of his jeans and the top of his sneakers. "I like short jeans," he told Jessie.

"Well, either you get new jeans or those jeans will soon look like shorts, not pants," Henry said, half joking. "Same with mine. I'm not much of a shopper, either, but sooner or later we all need new jeans."

The children walked over to the store next door. The Jeans Warehouse carried denim pants, jackets, shirts, and shorts. There were jeans stacked to the ceiling.

"How will we ever decide on jeans?" Violet asked. "The jeans store in Greenfield only has a few kinds."

"I'll help you," a smiling young woman

told Violet when she overheard her. "Tell me your sizes."

"We all need jeans," Jessie announced. "Here's a list of our sizes."

"Sure thing," the young woman said. "Why don't you each find a dressing room in back. I'll bring in some jeans for each of you."

The children found several empty dressing rooms and waited for the saleswoman. In a few minutes she came back with piles of jeans for the Aldens to try on. Jessie and Violet each found a pair right away.

"We're going to go pay for our jeans," Jessie told Henry as she stood outside his dressing room. "We'll be browsing around in the shops nearby. See you in a while."

Benny also decided on a pair quickly, the very first pair he tried. Jeans were jeans, and he wasn't going to try on any other pairs. He sat down in his dressing room to wait for Henry. He played with his coconut monkey and made funny faces in the dressing room mirror. "Next time, save your old jeans for me, okay?" he called over to

Henry in the next dressing room. "Then I won't have to go shopping again."

The boys stopped talking while Henry changed back into his regular clothes. That's how the boys happened to overhear two people talking just a ways down.

"I told you I don't want to get involved in this even to help you out," the young saleswoman said. "My boss said I can't hire anyone while she's away."

Henry and Benny heard the door to another dressing room bang shut. "I could work in the storeroom. I'm used to heavy lifting from my job on the boat."

"Sorry," the saleswoman said. "I'll let you know as soon as my boss comes back about whether we can hire you. Why don't you try some of the other stores."

"I . . . uh . . . well, I like this store, that's all," the man said.

Henry and Benny didn't hear anything else. They gathered up their new jeans and carried them to the cash register. While he waited to pay, Henry looked around the store. "That man's voice sounded familiar."

"Did you see who it was?" Benny asked.

"No, and now it's going to drive me bananas all day."

As they left the store, Benny suddenly felt empty-handed. "Uh-oh."

Henry looked down. "What's that *uh-oh* about?"

Benny's ears turned pink. He didn't want to tell Henry what had happened.

"My new coconut monkey! I think I left it in the dressing room when I was talking to you," Benny said.

"No problem. Just run back inside the store and get it," Henry said. "I'll wait right here."

When Benny came back, he was empty-handed again.

"What happened? Wasn't the monkey there?" Henry asked.

Benny swallowed hard. He wasn't going to cry, but he was upset with himself. After all, Henry had gone out and found him another monkey. Now it was lost again.

Henry went back inside to a clerk at the counter. "Did someone find a monkey in the dressing room?"

The clerk shook his head. "What an odd question! A monkey in the dressing room? How would a monkey get in there?"

The saleswoman came out of the dressing room area. She held up the coconut monkey. "Yip! Yip!" she said.

Benny ran toward the young woman. "Phew, I thought I lost this. Thank you."

"I saw you come in with it before, so I put it away when I found it. I knew you would come back," the woman said. "And the funny thing was, a man saw it and said it was his, but I didn't let him have it."

"Good thing," Henry said. "The one I bought at that other store was the last one in stock. Now, Benny, you'd better keep that next to you wherever you go."

Benny hugged his monkey. "I'll be really careful this time." With that, he put the coconut deep in his shopping bag. "Now nobody can see it."

CHAPTER 6

Locked In

After the boys met up with Jessie and Violet, they strolled along the glass balcony that overlooked the indoor food court in the mall.

Violet peeked over, then pulled back. "It makes me dizzy to look down."

"If I had my binoculars I could tell what everybody's eating from up here," Benny said, not dizzy at all. "This is a good spying spot."

Jessie laughed. "Well, I spy a soft-ice-cream stand down there. How about some ice cream before we go home? If we go right now, we should have just enough time to get some before the mall closes."

Benny raced over to the mall's glass elevator and pressed the button to go down. "Come on. Hurry up."

Moments later, the elevator glided to the ground floor and opened up onto the food court.

The children put their shopping bags down next to an empty table.

"I'll watch our stuff while you three get some ice cream," Henry said. "Would you bring me back a dish of chocolate?"

"Sure thing," Jessie said. "We'll be right back."

After Benny, Jessie, and Violet went off, Henry waited at their table and kept an eye on their belongings. Finally, he saw his brother and sisters carrying trays of ice-cream dishes. When the three children got closer, Henry ran up to help carry the trays back. "I'll get some napkins, too," Henry said.

Right then, a janitor pushed a cleaning

cart near the Aldens' table. The man checked all the nearby tables, picking up hats, bags, and items that people had left behind. At the very next table, he spotted one of the Aldens' shopping bags that had slipped onto the floor. The man picked it up and put it with all the other Lost and Found items on his cart.

The children returned with their ice cream and dug in.

A few minutes later, a voice interrupted them. "Attention, shoppers. The mall will be closing in fifteen minutes. Repeat. The mall will be closing in fifteen minutes."

The Aldens gathered their belongings. They brought their trays and empty dishes to the large garbage cans nearby.

"Now we can go home," Benny said. That's when he noticed that he was the only one without a shopping bag. "Do you have my jeans bag, Jessie?"

"No, there are only three bags," Jessie answered. "Where's yours?"

Benny pointed to the cleaning cart the worker had parked a few tables ahead.

"There it is, on top of that cart. I bet that cleaning man thought I left it behind, but I didn't." Benny ran ahead and tried to get the worker's attention. "That's my bag on your cart. I think you picked it up by mistake."

When the tall man turned around, Benny had a big surprise. "Mr. Merchant! Uh, that's my bag."

"Humph," Hap Merchant said when he saw Benny. "I can't just hand this over. These things are going to Lost and Found unless you can tell me what's inside."

"That's easy. My new jeans," Benny answered.

Hap opened the bag and checked inside. "Sorry," he said. "This bag must belong to someone else."

"Oh, right!" Benny added. "My coconut monkey, too."

Hap waited. Benny started to worry. "Isn't that what's inside? It's under the jeans."

"Humph," Hap repeated. Finally he handed the bag over to Benny.

"At least I didn't lose it this time," Benny said when he caught up with his brother and sisters. "Hap Merchant put it with all the other stuff people lost."

Jessie wondered about this. "Why would Hap be pushing around a cleaning cart? He manages the whole mall."

"He doesn't trust people, remember?" Violet said. "Martin Bolt told us he likes to do everything himself. He even does jobs for Penny's shop instead of letting us do them."

"He doesn't seem to want us working here, that's for sure," Henry said.

"He's always around when I have my monkey," Benny added. "Even when it's in a shopping bag."

Jessie took Benny's new jeans from his shopping bag and put them in another bag. "You know what? Let's take your monkey in this bag and put it away in Penny's store. That way you'll have it tomorrow when you and Henry take pirate pictures. We'll meet you by the exit door, okay?" Jessie said to Violet and Henry.

Shoppers scurried from the stores in the last few minutes. Jessie and Benny heard their footsteps echoing on the tile floors of the mall.

When the two children showed up at Penny's shop, Janet was in the back of the store, turning out the lights. "I thought you two were gone for the day."

"We were," Jessie said. "But I wanted to drop off something that we need tomorrow. Is that okay?"

Janet looked at her watch. "I guess so."

The children scooted over to the front of the store. Jessie found an empty shelf beneath the counter. She stuffed Benny's shopping bag behind a box on the shelf.

"Attention. The mall is closing in five minutes," Jessie and Benny heard on the loudspeaker.

"Let's hurry," Benny said. "I don't want to get locked in here by mistake."

"We'll take the glass elevator. It will take less time. 'Bye, Janet," Jessie called out.

No one answered.

"Janet?" Jessie said, louder this time.

Still no answer.

Benny took Jessie's outstretched hand. The store lights were going off all over the mall. Even Penny's Emporium was nearly dark, but the front door was still unlocked.

Jessie held Benny's hand tighter. "We can't leave until Janet gets back. The store's not locked. The gate isn't down. All the customers and shopkeepers are supposed to be gone by now. That's the rule. She must have gone down to the recycling room out back."

Jessie and Benny tiptoed to the back of the darkened store. There was no Janet. They looked in the storeroom. Still no Janet.

"I'll check the hallway behind the storeroom." Jessie stuck her head out the rear door of the storeroom. "I don't see or hear her. We can't go out this door because it will lock behind us."

"Should we call somebody?" Benny said.

"Let's go out into the mall," Jessie suggested. "Someone from the security staff is bound to come by."

The two children made their way through the darkened store. Benny bumped into a box.

Shkkk, shkkk, shkkk, the children heard next.

"What's that?" Benny gripped his sister's hand.

Jessie took a step and nearly fell down. "Popcorn!" she said, laughing a little. "That box you bumped into was full of popcorn kernels. They're all over the floor. I'll go get a broom and dustpan so no one else trips. Wait here."

"Can I come with you?" Benny asked.

Jessie took Benny's hand again. She didn't let go until they came back to sweep up the mess. "There. Let's put the broom and dustpan away and get out of here."

Benny and Jessie walked carefully now. They didn't want to knock over any more boxes or hear any more funny sounds.

When they reached the front of the store, they had another surprise, and not a popcorn surprise, either.

"The doors are locked!" Benny said.

Jessie tried to push the glass doors apart. "It's no use. Even if I force the doors open, the security gate is locked, too."

"Who locked us in?" Benny asked.

Jessie tugged at the door handles. "Janet must have still been in another part of the store, not in back. She probably didn't know we were inside, so she locked up."

Benny looked up at Jessie. "What are we going to do, Jessie?"

Before Jessie could answer, another unexpected sound startled the children.

"The phone's ringing!" Jessie said, relieved to hear the familiar sound. "Of course! We'll call security or Penny or somebody to come unlock us. But let me answer this call first."

Jessie picked up the phone. "Hello?"

"I'm on my way," a man's voice said.

The next sound Jessie heard was a click.

"Who was that?" Benny asked. "Is someone coming to get us?"

Jessie put down the phone. Her heart was pounding, but she tried not to let Benny see how nervous she was. "The person hung up."

The two children stood at the counter wondering what to do next. Suddenly a beam of light crisscrossed the store. Benny and Jessie ran to the front door.

"It's Janet!" Benny cried.

Janet unlocked the door and stepped inside. When she saw the two Aldens standing there, she jumped back. "How did you get in here?"

"I think you locked us in by mistake," Jessie explained. "We thought you were in the storeroom before, so we went back there. That must have been when you locked up. I'm sorry for all the confusion. Why did you come back?"

Janet didn't answer.

"Well, again, I'm sorry," Jessie went on. "I'm just glad you did return. I guess we'll go now."

Benny and Jessie slipped through the half-opened doors. The mall was deserted now. Hand in hand, Benny and Jessie walked quickly to the front exit door down-stairs.

A security man waved them out. "Come on, now. The stores are closed. Out you go."

Violet and Henry ran over, glad to see their brother and sister after the long wait.

"We almost gave up," Henry said. "What happened, anyway? You two are the last ones out."

But they were not the last ones out. Looking down on the Aldens from the top level of the glass balcony were two people who didn't seem in any hurry to leave.

CHAPTER 7

Sent Away

As soon as they arrived at Penny's Emporium the next morning, the Aldens heard popcorn popping. Penny stood at the cash register, ringing up a sale. When Janet saw the Aldens, she disappeared into the storeroom.

"I must say, she spends more time back there than out in the store sometimes," Penny told the Aldens. "Well, I'm glad you Aldens are here to lend a few hands again. I'm off to visit some of my suppliers today."

"What would you like us to do?" Jessie asked.

"You and Violet can stock the pushcart with some souvenir snow globes of Hope Harbor. People love those. Hap offered to bring up some shipments from the warehouse, but I'd rather send Henry down instead. Every time I turn around, Hap Merchant is in my way! As for Benny, he's my caramel corn man. I just made a batch that he can scoop into the boxes. If anybody comes in for pirate pictures, both boys can do that. See you in a few hours."

After Penny left, Jessie and Violet knocked on the storeroom door. They found Janet shaking the plastic snow globes and staring into each one.

"Penny said for us to put some of those out on the pushcart," Violet said, picking up one of the snow globes.

Janet looked cross. "Put that down. They're not ready to be sold yet. I have to check them first. Take some of those carved wooden boxes for the pushcart instead."

Jessie and Violet looked at each other.

Finally Jessie spoke up. "But . . . but Penny said — "

"Never mind what Penny said," Janet interrupted. "I'll explain to her about these later. Take the wooden boxes."

Jessie and Violet obeyed. Quietly they stocked the pushcart with wooden boxes, some souvenir pot holders, and some gift mugs. They pushed the cart into the mall area.

"I wonder why she was staring into all those snow globes," Violet said to Jessie.

Jessie sighed. "It doesn't matter. It's not worth arguing with Janet."

The girls were soon too busy to think about Janet. Inside the store, Benny filled up caramel corn boxes. When he was done, he went over to help Henry with the pirate photos.

"Go back and ask Janet to give you some film from the storeroom. There's none left here," Henry told Benny.

Janet didn't like being interrupted. "What are you doing here?" she asked Benny when he entered the storeroom. "I thought Penny wanted you to fill up the popcorn boxes."

Benny gulped. He never seemed to say the right thing around this young woman. "I finished that already. Henry said to ask you something." He took a deep breath but no words came out.

Janet shoved some boxes onto a shelf. "Well, what do you want? I'm very busy."

"Henry says he needs film," Benny said quickly. "There's no more in the camera."

"Well, tell him he'll have to go to Fast Photo to pick up some more film."

At that moment, the back door to the storeroom opened. The young crewman from the docks stood there looking at Benny, then at Janet.

"I . . . uh . . . guess I came in the wrong way again," the young man said. "I'll go around and come in the front way."

Janet stood up. "Never mind. You can go through here."

The crewman stepped over the boxes in the storeroom. Janet and Benny trailed after him into the shop.

Janet went straight over to Henry. "I

need the four of you to run errands for me.
First, get some film from Fast Photo. Just
charge it to the shop."

Jessie decided to speak up. "Are you sure
all four of us have to go, Janet? Penny asked
us to help sell things from the pushcart.
You'll be the only one in the store."

Janet put her hands on her hips. "I've
done it before. In fact, covering the shop by
myself is easier than supervising new people. If you really want to help out, then
please pick up what I need." With that,
Janet turned away from the children.

"Those two seem to know each other,"
Violet whispered to Jessie, "but they act like
strangers when we're around."

"Know what?" Benny asked, whispering.
"That man came in the storeroom again by
mistake."

"I noticed that," Jessie said. "Customers
aren't supposed to use the back entrance. I
wonder how he got in. You need a key to
the back staircase."

When Janet saw the children whispering,

she came over to them again. "If all you're doing is standing around talking, then do it during the errands I asked you to do."

"First, I'm going down to the warehouse to pick up those boxes Penny told me about," Henry said.

"What boxes?" Janet demanded.

"Hap told Penny there were deliveries for the shop that arrived," Henry explained. "I was going to pick them up now, then go on your errands."

Janet wasn't having any of this. "I'm afraid my errands are more urgent. I'll make other arrangements for someone to pick up those boxes. Now, all of you, please get going."

"Whew, I wish people would make up their minds," Henry said after the children left the store. "Penny tells us one thing, then when she's gone, Janet wants something else."

Jessie frowned. "You know what I've noticed? Janet never wants Henry to pick up shipments when she's around."

Henry shrugged. "Well, she's in charge whenever Penny's gone, so I guess we should do what she says."

Before he left with Henry and his sisters, Benny remembered something. "Well, I'm bringing my monkey with me. I don't want to leave it here anymore."

Benny went to fetch his monkey from under the counter.

"I thought you left," Janet said.

Benny scooted past the young woman. "I forgot something."

Jessie followed Benny behind the counter. Bending down, Jessie slid her hand back and forth over the shelf where she and Benny had hidden the bag. "Benny, you didn't move the bag this morning, did you?"

Now Benny scooted behind the counter. "Don't worry, Jessie. It's behind a box. I know it's there. I'll get it."

But when Benny moved the box, he discovered the space behind it was totally empty.

CHAPTER 8

Locked Out

"Well, don't look at me. I don't know why you leave things lying around if they're so important." Janet thumbed through some sales slips as if nothing had happened. "Anyway, I need you to do those errands if you're going to be working tonight," Janet said as she walked into the storeroom.

"Why don't you and Benny stay here," Henry suggested to Jessie, "while Violet and I do the errands. We'll get back lickety-split to help you look for your monkey."

After Violet and Henry left, Jessie and Benny searched Penny's shop high and low. The only monkey they found was a little one hanging from a plastic tree.

"I know I put it under the counter," Benny said. "It couldn't just walk away." Benny crinkled his forehead. "Penny told Mrs. Frye she likes it when I make people laugh with my monkey faces while Henry takes pirate pictures."

"Which we can't do until your brother and sister get back with the film, by the way," Janet said as she approached Jessie. "Well, as long as you're here, cover the shop for a while. You'll have to hunt for Benny's toy later. Right now, I have to pick up those shipments Penny mentioned."

Several customers came into the store. There was no more time to be upset or to hunt for a lost coconut monkey.

About twenty minutes later, Janet returned.

Benny tiptoed over to the storeroom to see what she was up to. "Janet locked some boxes in the closet," he whispered to Jessie

when he returned. "What if it's those coconuts Penny ordered?"

Jessie hated to see the disappointment on
Benny's face. "Maybe Penny can set aside
one of them for you if yours doesn't turn
up. We'll ask Penny about it when she gets
back. I don't want to bother Janet anymore."

An hour later Violet and Henry returned.

"Did you find Benny's lost monkey?" Violet asked.

Benny shook his head. "It's missing, not
lost. We put it under the counter. Now it's
not there."

Then Benny had an idea. "You know how
Henry threw out my monkey at the picnic
area? Maybe this one got thrown out by
mistake, too. Don't some of the cleaning
people come by after the store closes?"

The older children weren't too sure
about this. Still, it couldn't hurt to look
through the trash.

"I told Penny I'd take some empty cardboard boxes down to the recycling bins,"
Henry said. "Right before closing time, why

don't we all go to the recycling area and search down there for Benny's monkey."

Penny called half an hour before closing time. "Penny says you can leave," Janet told the children after she hung up the phone. "She was delayed and asked me to close up the shop."

"Sure thing," Henry said. "We're going to the recycling room to dump all these empty cardboard boxes. Is that okay?"

Janet didn't answer right away. "I guess so. I'll help you out."

"That's okay. They're easy to carry," Henry said.

Janet followed the Aldens out anyway. She didn't go back to the shop until the elevator doors closed.

When the elevator doors opened again, the Aldens stepped into the large, empty recycling room.

"Hello!" Henry yelled.

"Hello!" Henry's voice echoed right back.

"It's kind of creepy down here," Benny said. "Can we look real fast, then go?"

"Let's stick together," Henry said. "We'll dump these boxes into this cardboard recycling bin, then do a quick look around for your monkey."

After the children dumped their boxes, Jessie pointed to another bin ahead. "Look, that one says '*P.E.*' That must be where the paper trash from Penny's Emporium goes."

Henry and Jessie got to work. Both of them carefully lifted out sales slips, wrappings, and other kinds of paper. Jessie and Henry reached the bottom of the bin.

"There are lots of papers and empty bags, but no shopping bag with a coconut monkey inside," Henry told Benny.

Jessie slowly put the wastepaper from Penny's shop back into the bin again. The last bunch of papers she picked up was a thick stack of forms that looked clean and smooth.

"Hey, wait!" she said. "I don't think these shipping orders belong here. Penny saves all of them to match up with the bills that come in with her shipments."

Shipping orders in hand, the Aldens

walked over to the elevator. They watched the floor numbers above the doors. None of them lit up.

"What's wrong, Henry?" Benny asked. "How come it's taking so long to come down here?"

"Maybe the freight elevator doesn't run after the mall closes," Henry said. "I didn't realize it was so late. We'd better try the stairs."

But when the children climbed the stairs, they found that all the doors leading to the mall were locked.

The stairwell was dark. Only the glow of the exit signs gave off any light at all.

"Hello! Hello!" Jessie called out.

"Hello! Hello!" her voice echoed back.

"Let's at least get up to the level where Penny's shop is. Maybe we can get the attention of the security people by banging on the door. They're bound to go by sooner or later."

Jessie and Henry took turns looking out the small window on the stairwell door. A couple of times, they saw security people go

by on their motorcarts. But they were too far away to hear or see the children.

A very long time went by. To pass the time, Violet told the story of Corduroy, the toy bear in a department store.

Just when Jessie wondered if anyone would come by, she spotted someone approaching.

"It's Hap," she said. "He's coming out of Penny's shop. Isn't that odd? The store is closed now. Why would he be in there?"

Jessie banged on the door and yelled, "Hap! Hap!"

Hap heard the banging and looked around. He couldn't tell where the noise was coming from. He boarded his motorcart and started to drive away.

Jessie banged again, louder this time. Hap stopped the cart and got off. Jessie waved in the small window of the heavy metal door. She banged and banged again to get Hap's attention.

"He heard me!" she told her brothers and sister.

Hap unlocked the door and found the children on the other side of it.

"Thank goodness you heard us," Jessie told Hap. "We got locked in the recycling room after hours. The only way we could get out was up the stairs. But these doors were locked."

Hap was not as glad to see the Aldens as they were to see him. In fact, Hap looked downright angry. "The doors are locked to keep people out of the mall after hours."

The children looked down at their feet. They knew they didn't belong in the mall after it closed. Why did they always seem like such nuisances around Hap?

"We're sorry," Jessie said. "We were looking for something Benny lost."

"Not that blasted monkey?" Hap asked.

"We found some missing papers." Henry held up Penny's shipping orders.

"I'll take those," Hap said, taking the papers from Henry. "What was Mr. Bolt thinking when he invited kids to work like they were grown-ups? Well, it's a wonder this mall runs at all."

Hap walked the children to an exit door that led outside. "Now, go home. No dilly-dallying."

The children stepped into the cool night air. There were still tourists walking around on the docks, having a good time. But tonight the Aldens didn't feel like carefree tourists, just very tired children who needed to go home.

CHAPTER 9

Benny Sneezes

When the children came down to breakfast the next day, they were sleepier than usual. They were quieter than usual, too.

Mrs. Frye tried to perk them up. "Have some of my famous blueberry pancakes. Those will wake you up."

Henry dug into a stack of pancakes. "These are delicious. We sometimes make these when Mrs. McGregor, our house-keeper, has a day off."

Mrs. Frye refilled the milk pitcher. "And

when will you children get a day off to be plain old slugabeds?"

Henry poured himself another glass of milk. "Maybe when Grandfather gets back. Penny needs us today. It's Janet Trainor's day off. We won't be seeing her today."

When the children arrived at the mall, they had some extra time to go window-shopping. They strolled through the far end of the mall, where they hadn't visited before.

Benny finally visited the train store. Henry and Jessie stopped to check out tents at a camping store. Violet browsed through a shop that sold nothing but beads. She bought a small bag of them along with some cord to make a necklace for Mrs. Frye.

As he strolled along, Benny stared up at the huge round skylight at the top of the mall. "This mall is humongous," he said.

"It sure is." Jessie took hold of Benny's hand. She didn't want him to bump into anyone while he was staring at the ceiling.

"We've only seen about half the shops, too."

The children stopped in front of the South Seas Shop.

"Maybe they sell things from Hawaii," Violet said.

Jessie looked closely in the window. "They do, but only expensive things, like fabrics and jewelry and antiques from the Pacific Islands."

This made Benny think about his missing coconut monkey. Even though the South Seas Shop didn't look like the kind of store that sold anything like that, he peeked in anyway.

Jessie followed Benny and also peeked in. There, standing at the cash register, was Janet Trainor.

"Hi, Janet," Jessie said, stepping into the store. "You work here, too?"

Janet's face turned almost as pink as the hot pink fabric on display behind her. "Uh, well, yes. I do work here part-time on my days off. I'm . . . uh . . . saving money to go back to college, so I need two jobs."

Henry wondered about this. "Wouldn't Penny give you more hours if you wanted them? We're going back to Greenfield soon, so there will be a lot of work to do."

Janet said nothing. At that moment, a man came up to the cash register to pay for a Hawaiian shirt. Janet turned away from the Aldens and didn't speak to them again.

"Should we mention to Penny that Janet works here?" Henry asked his brother and sisters when they left the store.

Jessie thought about this. "Why not? If Penny knew Janet needed money for school, she might offer her more hours to work."

By this time, the Aldens were in front of Penny's Emporium. Penny waved the children over. She held up the stack of shipping orders the children had found the night before. "Hap dropped these shipping orders off with a note. He said you children found them in the recycling center. Did you throw them away by mistake?"

Henry shook his head. "No, we were

looking for Benny's monkey — it's missing again. We wondered whether it might have gone out with the trash by mistake. While we were looking for it, we found the slips in the recycling bin. Hap took them from us. I guess he didn't trust that we'd give them to you."

Penny smiled. "Don't be afraid of Hap. He's always poking around here to fix problems. I wish he could fix the problem I have now, though."

"What is it?" Jessie asked.

"For the life of me, I can't locate the shipments that go with these slips. They're for the coconut monkeys." Penny scratched her head. "Well, I'll have to ask Janet when she comes back to work. She's never around when I need her — always up to something else instead of what needs doing."

"Like working in another shop," Benny blurted out. When he saw Jessie's eyes open like saucers, he covered his mouth. "Oops."

Penny stared at Benny. "Janet is working in another shop? Which one?"

"The South Seas Shop," Henry answered. "She said she needed another job to save money for school."

Penny looked totally confused now. "I've offered her more hours, but she told me she didn't have time." Penny bit her lip. "Perhaps she doesn't like working for me."

The Aldens looked at one another. What could be more fun than working for Penny?

Penny picked up the shipping orders. "Well, I've got to track down the shipments that go with these slips. I'm going to double-check the storeroom one last time."

That's when Benny almost jumped up and down. "Know what? Know what?" he asked Penny. "Janet put some boxes in the closet and locked it. We saw her, didn't we, Jessie?"

Jessie nodded. "Good for you, Benny. I forgot about that. Maybe the missing monkeys are in the boxes!"

The children followed Penny into the storeroom. Penny took out the keys she carried around on her belt loop. She unlocked the closet, hoping to find her missing shipments. But when she opened the door, the shelves were completely empty.

"Where did those boxes go?" Penny asked, looking at Benny. "You actually saw her put them in there, right?"

"Lots of boxes," Benny said, very sure of himself.

Penny shut the door. "No point in locking the closet. The shipments aren't there. Now, why on earth did Janet lock those monkeys anyway? She knew I wanted to put them out in the store right away."

The Aldens followed Penny out to the shop.

"Uh-oh," Violet said. "There's that man again from the freighter. Whenever he's here, he never looks like he's shopping."

Jessie walked over to him. "May I help you?" she asked the young man.

"I was wondering if the store manager was here," the man answered. "She was . . . uh . . . helping me pick out some presents the other day, but I had to leave."

Jessie nodded toward Penny. "There she is. I'll call her over."

The young man frowned. "Not her."

"You mean Janet," Jessie said. "She's at the South Seas Shop today. She'll be back in here tomorrow, I think."

Without even saying thank you, the young man left.

Jessie didn't have time to tell the other children or Penny about the crewman. Several tour groups were visiting Hope Harbor. Most of them wanted souvenirs and pirate photos of themselves.

When five o'clock rolled around, Jessie had forgotten about the crewman's visit. Penny shooed the Aldens away. "It's time for fun. You've worked long enough. Hap Merchant is coming by the shop to help me out. You know how he is around children, even nice ones like you Aldens. Now go off and have a good time."

"A good time for me would be finding my monkey," Benny said to the other children as they left the store. "Can we go to that shop with the Hawaiian stuff? Maybe they have things made out of coconuts."

The older children thought this was un-likely, but they decided to go to the shop anyway.

Although it was only five o'clock, the South Seas Shop was dark when the chil-dren arrived.

"That sign says, 'Closed Until Seven,' " Henry said.

Benny pushed the door open anyway. "I don't think it's closed."

The Aldens followed Benny. At first they didn't see any customers or salespeople.

"Come on, let's go," Henry whispered. "Nobody's here."

"Shhh," Jessie said. "Somebody is here. Listen."

When the children stood still, they heard soft murmuring voices coming from the back of the shop. They tiptoed in a few steps more.

Violet pointed. "Look back there."

Huddled around a small table were three people. One of them was a man wearing big magnifying glasses like jewelers wore.

"It's Janet and the crewman from the

freighter," Henry said. "The other person must be the store owner. I can't tell what they're looking at."

Benny grabbed Henry's arm and pointed to his nose. He was about to sneeze!

Henry took Benny's hand. Violet and Jessie followed them.

Too late!

"Kerchew! Kerchew!"

The Aldens galloped from the store. When Jessie turned around, she saw three people at the table squinting. Thank goodness the close-up spotlight over the table blinded them from recognizing the Aldens.

Henry led the other three children out a back door. They were in the hallway now, behind the South Seas Shop.

"Whew, that was close," Henry said.

"Sorry I had to sneeze," Benny said. "The more I tried not to sneeze, the more I had to."

"I couldn't tell what they were looking at, could you?" Henry asked.

"It looked like they had a bunch of old,

dusty pebbles," Benny said. "Hey, look, the back door to the shop is open."

Henry pushed the door gently.

The storeroom was filled with bolts of fabric, masks from the Polynesian islands, and antiques from around the world.

"Hey, look at these!" Jessie said when she nearly knocked over a stack of boxes. "The label says, 'Penny's Emporium.' "

The Aldens knew what to do. These were Penny's boxes, and they were in the wrong place. Without saying anything, each child took a couple of boxes, except for Benny, who could manage only one.

"These boxes didn't just walk here," Jessie said, tiptoeing into the hallway with the boxes in her arms. "Either Janet or that crewman moved them from Penny's storeroom."

"It had to be Janet," Henry said, gently closing the door behind him. "Let's face it, every time there was a shipment coming to Penny's shop, she tried to get it before anyone else. I don't know how that crewman from the freighter figures in, but he and Janet know each other better than they let on."

Jessie took out the Swiss Army knife she always carried in her pocket. She opened one of the boxes.

"Omigosh!" she said, startled at the sight of rows of smiling monkey faces staring back at her. "These are the Hawaiian coconuts Penny ordered."

Benny couldn't get over seeing so many coconut monkeys in one place. "Is mine there?"

Henry opened the other boxes. All of them were filled with coconuts just like the ones Benny had lost. "Well, if yours isn't in here, there are lots of others just like them. Janet and that crewman must be looking for something inside these coconuts."

"Maybe one of them took Benny's monkey to see if there was something inside it," Violet said. "Janet was always around when Benny's coconut was around. And she was gone a lot when his coconut was gone."

Benny could hardly catch his breath.

"Don't forget Hap. He had my monkey in the cleaning cart."

Jessie replaced the box lid. "You're right. And he never seemed to want us getting the shipments, either. Anyway, we'd better get these back — "

Suddenly a spot of light blinded Jessie. Then, one by one, it blinded the other children.

"What are you doing here?" a booming voice called out.

When the flashlight finally went off, the Aldens found themselves staring up at a very angry Hap Merchant.

"You children don't belong here. And these boxes don't belong to you, either. Why did you bring them here?"

Without waiting for an answer, Hap went over to a storage closet in the hallway. He came back with a hand truck. "Stack those boxes here. These are going back to Penny's. I'll have to tell her what you've been up to."

"But . . . but — " Jessie began.

"No buts about it," Hap said. "Penny was

missing these shipments, and you had them."

With that, Hap pushed the hand truck down the hall. He hit the freight elevator button. When the elevator arrived, he rolled the hand truck inside. The doors closed, and Hap and dozens of coconut monkeys disappeared into the depths of the mall.

CHAPTER 10

Monkey Business

The children had called Mrs. Frye to let her know that they would be home soon. Since Janet and Hap didn't want the Aldens around, it wasn't as much fun visiting Hope Harbor Mall anymore.

As the children walked along Waterfront Street, Benny noticed his grandfather's car parked up ahead. "Grandfather's back from his trip," he said.

This cheered up all the children.

"We can have dinner together," Violet said. "There's a lot to tell him. This visit didn't turn out to be the way we thought it would."

As the children drew closer to Mr. Bolt's house, their grandfather came out of the house.

Benny skipped ahead to get the first hug. "Grandfather! You're back."

Mr. Alden couldn't put out his arms to hug Benny. He was holding something he had found on the front steps of Mr. Bolt's house, something round and hairy.

"My monkey!" Benny cried when he noticed what Mr. Alden had in his hands. "Where did you get it?"

Mr. Alden read a note taped to the monkey:

"Dear Benny,
I found out this belonged to you after I found it at the mall. I hope you are glad to get it back.
A Friend"

Grandfather Alden then said, "Goodness, Benny, how did your monkey get all the way from that garbage truck to Mr. Bolt's house?"

Benny hugged the monkey to his chest. "Oh, this isn't the one I lost. I mean, well, I lost this one, too, but it's a new one."

One by one, the other children came up to their grandfather for hugs.

"I have a feeling there's a story that goes with that monkey," Mr. Alden said. "First I found it on these steps with a note. Now Benny says this monkey isn't the one that was missing. Would somebody tell me what has been going on while Martin and I were gone?"

By this time, Martin Bolt had come outside to help with the luggage. He looked just as confused as Mr. Alden when the children began to tell them about the last few days. "Goodness, I'm sorry you children had such a rough time of it. Nothing exciting ever happens when I'm there."

Benny smiled up at his grandfather's old friend. "Oh, we had a good time, but sometimes not. Anyway, we like it when exciting things happen."

Mr. Bolt smiled at this. "Listen, now that we've unpacked the car, I'd like to go back to the mall. Then we can have a late dinner there."

Benny tilted his head to look at Jessie's watch. "The mall closes in a while. We can't stay there because Hap doesn't like that. It's the rule."

Now Mr. Bolt threw his head back and laughed. "That's my rule! But since I own the mall, I think we can break that rule tonight."

Benny's face lit up. "Goody! Now nobody can kick us out."

The children walked back to the mall with their grandfather and Mr. Bolt. They told them more about the mysterious happenings.

"Here's a mystery," Jessie said. "Who returned Benny's second monkey?"

Benny shook the monkey to hear it rattle. "Know what? This coconut Grandfather found doesn't rattle. It's empty."

Henry picked it up. "Hey, this isn't the one I gave you, Benny, just one that looks like it. Now things are getting stranger than ever."

"Your grandfather and I have a few calls to make in my office," Mr. Bolt said. "You children can come up now or hang around the mall for a half hour until we're finished. What do you say?"

The Aldens weren't children who liked to hang around when they had to finish solving a mystery.

"We're going to find out who left this monkey at your house," Benny said.

The other children nodded in agreement. They were going to get to the bottom of this.

Their first stop was Penny's store. When they showed up, Hap and Janet were standing outside the shop, arguing. They grew silent when they noticed the Aldens staring at them.

"I think I left something in the storeroom," Jessie told Janet. "We'll only be a minute."

Before Janet could answer, the children walked briskly through Penny's shop and went straight to the storeroom.

"There are the monkey boxes," Henry

said. "Hap must have brought them back here. But it looks as if some of the coconuts are missing from the boxes. I bet the one Grandfather found with the note came from here."

"Hey, I just remembered something," Benny said. He reached into his jeans pocket and pulled out the note he had found at the restaurant. It was wrinkled, but he could still see the handwriting. "It's the same as the handwriting on the monkey note. Maybe Janet wrote it, even though these aren't her initials."

"Or that crewman," Violet said. "Remember, he was at the restaurant with Janet, too?"

"Are you talking about me?" Janet said, standing in the doorway. "And why are you shaking those?" she asked when she saw Benny pick up each coconut and shake it.

"To see if they make noise," Benny said. "The one I lost made noise, but this one doesn't. It's not the same one."

The Aldens were shaking all the coconuts now.

"None of these make noise," Jessie said. "Where are all the other ones that were in these boxes?"

Janet was about to answer when the back door of the storeroom opened. The young crewman stood in the doorway. In his arms were two boxes of plastic souvenir snow globes. "Oops," he said. "Wrong door."

Henry stepped forward. "No, it's the right door, and you know it's the right door. We've already figured out that you and Janet know each other and that you've been coming to the storeroom on purpose. The only thing we don't know is why."

"Maybe you can start out by explaining why you have those snow globes," Jessie said. "They belong to Penny, and there's no reason you should have them. But you do."

Janet and the young man looked at each other.

Benny took the wrinkled note and showed it to the crewman. "Did you write this note?" Then he held up the other note. "And this one?"

The crewman looked at Janet. The storeroom was so quiet everyone could hear one another breathing.

That's when Penny appeared in the doorway. "Everybody come out here. Mr. Bolt, Hap, and Mr. Alden are here. We all have a lot of questions to ask."

Janet and the crewman stepped back.

"We have other things to do," Janet told Penny.

Jessie slipped behind Janet, blocking the door.

"Something odd has been going on with my shipments," Penny said. "Before I call in the customs inspectors to look things over, I want to give you a chance to tell me why things have been missing from my shop. I've locked the shop for now, so we don't have to worry about being interrupted."

Janet and the crewman exchanged glances.

Janet looked up. "I guess I'll go first. First of all, this is my brother, Robert Trainor. He's been working on a freighter for the last six months to pay back some debts."

Robert Trainor looked around the room

at all the upset faces. "I'd better tell this part, so my sister doesn't get blamed for everything. I got involved with some people who were trying to smuggle some antique counting stones back from the South Seas. They're marked pebbles people used a long time ago to figure out math problems. They are quite valuable to collectors. But they're even more valuable to the people on those islands. They were stolen from a museum."

"Did you take them?" Mr. Alden asked.

"No!" Janet interrupted. "Robert isn't good with money, but he's not a thief."

The crewman shook his head. "No, I'm not a thief, but I might as well be. I guess I'm just not too smart. I got a job on a freighter and learned there were smugglers on board. They found out my sister worked at a shop in Hope Harbor where the boat was coming in. They hid the counting stones in some of the shipments that were coming here. They figured if anyone got caught, it would be Janet, not them and me. I should have reported them right away when I discovered what they were doing, but I was afraid. I just went along with everything until the ship pulled into Hope Harbor."

"My coconut!" Benny cried. "Were those counting stones inside my monkey?"

For the first time, both Janet and Robert Trainor almost smiled.

"No. But we did check all the coconut monkeys we could track down," Janet explained. "Some just had nutshells inside to make noise. A few of them had the smuggled counting stones. But not yours, Benny, not even the one I took from under the counter."

Robert Trainor picked up where his sister left off. "See, the smugglers hid the stones inside some of the monkeys and some of those plastic snow globes. Janet and I tried to look through all of them so we could return them to the museum." Robert paused and looked at Martin Bolt. "Call up Mr. Hana, the owner of the South Seas Shop. He'll tell you how we tried to get the stones back to their rightful place. Honest."

"I know Mr. Hana quite well," Martin Bolt said. "I'll call him right now."

While Mr. Bolt made his phone call in the back of the store, Benny looked at his silent coconut. "What happened to the one I had that did rattle?"

Janet lowered her eyes. "We cracked it, trying to find out what was inside. So we replaced it with another one. But we forgot to pick one that rattled. I know I wasn't nice to you, but it was because I was afraid my brother would be arrested with the smugglers. Every time Robert and I tried to check the shipments, the four of you would show up. I even came back here the night you got locked in Penny's shop."

Jessie looked at Robert. "Were you the person who called the shop that night, then hung up?"

Robert nodded. "Yes. I thought it was Janet answering, so I came over. We returned to the mall after it was closed and waited for you to leave. I even tried to get a job at the jeans store because you kids were making it so hard for me and Janet to check shipments together. I found your monkey in the jeans store, but the saleswoman took it away."

Penny Block looked upset now. "Janet, I don't understand some things. Why did you go off to work in another shop?"

"I'm sorry," Janet apologized. "I thought if I got to know Mr. Hana, he could help us find out how to return the counting stones to the museum. We're not criminals."

By this time, Martin Bolt had rejoined everyone. "These two young people are not only not criminals," he announced, "they risked their safety tracking down the counting stones before the smugglers could claim them. When Mr. Hana heard their story, he called the customs inspectors. He just told me they found one box in a secret hiding place on the ship."

"The trapdoor I saw!" Benny shouted.

"Quite right, Benny," Martin Bolt said. "Mr. Hana has been working with the authorities. He advised Robert to leave one box on the ship. The inspectors boarded the ship and ordered the smugglers to open the trapdoor. Only this time, the smugglers were trapped!"

Everyone stopped talking when they heard someone banging on the door to Penny's shop.

Penny went to the front door. Hap was standing there knocking on the door. "That Hap. He's always around just when I don't need him to be," Penny whispered. "I'd better explain what's happening, or he'll just burst right through those doors."

"You're supposed to be open, Penny," Hap said, stepping into the shop. "Anything wrong around here? I hope that young woman didn't tell you about the tiff we had. I found out she was the one who threw out your shipping orders so you wouldn't know about some missing shipments. Good thing you have me around to keep an eye on things."

"We thought you had something to do with Penny's missing shipments," Henry confessed to Hap.

"And my monkey!" Benny interrupted. "Don't forget my monkey. It was on the cleaning cart the other night, and Hap wouldn't give it back."

Mr. Bolt stood in front of Hap. "Were you cleaning up the food court again, Hap? This isn't the job of my chief manager, you know. Not to mention trying to run Penny's shop half the time. I need you for the big jobs. These other folks can do the other jobs."

Hap looked at Penny. Everyone noticed his ears getting as pink as could be. "Well, I like helping Penny, but I can't get her to help me back."

Penny looked at Hap for a long time. "What do you mean?"

"By keeping me company once in a while," Hap confessed. "Until these Alden kids showed up, Penny and I were getting to know each other pretty well. Then they had to take up all her time with those monkeys and such. I haven't got a chance with these noisy kids around."

Penny smiled at Hap as if she were seeing him for the first time. "Well, if you like me, then you'd better get used to noisy kids. I plan to ask the Aldens to come back to Hope Harbor Mall anytime they want. They're good for my business."

"Good for your monkey business, you mean," Benny said.

GERTRUDE CHANDLER WARNER discovered when she was teaching that many readers who like an exciting story could find no books that were both easy and fun to read. She decided to try to meet this need, and her first book, *The Boxcar Children*, quickly proved she had succeeded.

Miss Warner drew on her own experiences to write the mystery. As a child she spent hours watching trains go by on the tracks opposite her family home. She often dreamed about what it would be like to set up housekeeping in a caboose or freight car — the situation the Alden children find themselves in.

When Miss Warner received requests for more adventures involving Henry, Jessie, Violet, and Benny Alden, she began additional stories. In each, she chose a special setting and introduced unusual or eccentric characters who liked the unpredictable.

While the mystery element is central to each of Miss Warner's books, she never thought of them as strictly juvenile mysteries. She liked to stress the Aldens' independence and resourcefulness and their solid New England devotion to using up and making do. The Aldens go about most of their adventures with as little adult supervision as possible — something else that delights young readers.

Miss Warner lived in Putnam, Connecticut, until her death in 1979. During her lifetime, she received hundreds of letters from girls and boys telling her how much they liked her books.